Kill Swap

by

James Lovegrove

First published in 2007 in Great Britain by
Barrington Stoke Ltd
18 Walker St, Edinburgh, EH3 7LP

www.barringtonstoke.co.uk

ISBN 978-1-84299-447-4

Printed in Great Britain by Bell & Bain Ltd

A Note from the Author

I don't want to say too much about *Kill Swap* here. The plot has a few "twists" and I don't want to give them away.

I had the idea for the story while I was lying awake in bed late one night, or rather, early one morning. Strange thoughts come into my head at 4 a.m. when the house is silent and the world is dark.

"Suppose you had to kill someone you had never met," I said to myself. "What would be a good reason to do that?"

Kill Swap is one answer to that question.

To Lou, Monty and Theo,
with love

Contents

Chapter 1
Killer In The Bushes

It was 7.25 p.m. The evening was cold and the sky was dark.

I had been crouching in the bushes for almost an hour. I was freezing, damp and stiff.

The windows were lit up in the houses across the road from me. Between the leaves of the bushes I could see people indoors. They were eating their dinner and watching TV. All of the houses were big and posh. The families who lived in them looked happy and content. The cars parked outside were fancy ones. This was a smart, rich part of the city, not like where I lived.

One house had no lights on. The person who lived there hadn't come home yet.

But he would soon. In less than five minutes.

I checked the gun in my hand. The number on the barrel had been rubbed off. There was thick brown parcel tape wrapped around the grip. I would tear that off later on. I didn't want my fingers to leave any prints on the gun. If the police ever found the gun, they would never know where it had come from or who had fired it.

The first bullet was ready in the chamber.

My target was a rich man who worked in London. He took the train there and back every day. He made lots of money as a banker and helped other people make lots of money too. He always got home at exactly 7.30 p.m. every week day. He had no wife and no children. That was all I knew about him.

At 7.30 p.m. on the dot, his car came round the corner at the end of the street. It was a big BMW. He drove it to and from the station. It slid to a halt outside the house that had no lights on. The engine stopped and the man got out.

He was thin, sleek, and well dressed. He beeped the car's alarm and walked to the steps of his house.

I crept out from where I was hidden in the bushes, in a small park across the road from the man's house. I left the park and walked quickly towards the man. I had pulled the hood of my hoodie up over my head. I was holding the gun tightly in my right hand and my hand was hidden inside my hoodie. No one could see the gun.

I didn't even know my target's name.

All I knew was that he had to die.

Tonight I was going to kill someone I had never met.

Chapter 2
£8,000

Two weeks before, my dad had got into trouble. Serious trouble.

Dad liked to bet a lot on the horses, and he almost always lost. Most of his spare money went on horse races. So did most of the money that was for our food and the other things we needed. It used to drive my mum crazy.

"How can you do this to us, Mick?" she shouted at him one day. "How can you keep throwing all our money away like this? Jack needs clothes and things for school. We need to buy food."

"Just you wait," Dad replied. "One of these days I'll win big. Really big. Then you'll see. My luck's going to change. It *has* to change. And then we'll have plenty of food, and Jack won't have to worry about clothes or anything. We'll have a proper car, not that crappy old banger any more. You can buy yourself some nice shoes, my love. Jack can get a PlayStation and one of those 'G-3 razor phones' or whatever they're called."

"I've heard all that before," Mum said with a sigh. "You promise all this stuff, and it never happens. You just lose more money and we end up poorer than ever."

"I mean it this time," Dad insisted. "Just wait a little bit longer. Trust me."

That argument wasn't too bad. But the times when my dad lost a lot of money at the bookies, then he'd go to the pub and get drunk. He'd stagger home, and he and Mum would scream at each other long into the night. Neighbours rang the police sometimes. It scared me and I was embarrassed. Everyone in our block of flats knew us as the "rough" family. We got called *troublemakers* and *shocking*, and a lot of things that weren't even as polite as that!

Dad's gambling got worse, and he needed more cash. So he went to a man called Tony Mullen for a loan. He borrowed £8,000 off Mullen. But Dad didn't use the loan to pay off what he owed to the bookies. He gambled with it instead. He thought he could turn the £8,000 into more money by betting with it. He quickly lost it all.

When he told Mum, she went mental.

"Tony Mullen!" she yelled. "Tony bloody Mullen! He's only the biggest crook on the estate, and you owe him £8,000?"

"Plus interest," Dad said softly.

"He'll kill you. Do you know that? If you can't pay him back, Mullen will kill you. Or break your legs at the very least. Mick, you truly are an idiot, and I'm sorry I ever married you and had your son."

"Forgive me, Karen. Please," Dad begged.

"Too late," said my mum. "Get out. Get out of our flat and don't come back."

She chucked Dad out. He went off with a carrier bag that had some of his clothes in and a toothbrush. That was all.

He looked pathetic as he walked away with his carrier bag. He looked like a dog that had been kicked.

Chapter 3

The Man With The Missing Tooth

A week after Dad left, a man rang our doorbell.

He had a bald head and a gold stud in one ear. He was dressed in a tracksuit, and one of his front teeth was missing. His arms and hands were massive, like a gorilla's.

"Is Mick in?" he asked as if he was one of Dad's mates. But we knew he wasn't.

"You're one of Tony Mullen's boys, aren't you?" my mum replied. She was scared but she was trying not to show it.

"I work for Mr Mullen, yes."

"Then you can tell your boss I've thrown my husband out. I've no idea where he is now."

The man leaned into our flat from the doorway. He saw me sitting on the sofa and gave me a big grin – the sort of grin that isn't friendly at all.

"All right?" he said to me.

I nodded. I didn't like the way he looked at me.

"Don't you talk to Jack," Mum said to him. "I've told you I don't know where Mick is. Now go. Please."

She gave the man a prod in the chest, trying to get him to move back outside the flat.

The man didn't like this. He looked hard at Mum as if she had punched him, not just given him a small push.

"Now that was rude," he said. "Here I am, being ever so polite. Why do you have to go and get all aggressive with me?"

He grabbed my mum's arms and shoved her backwards. She staggered, tripped, and fell on the floor. The man towered over her. He had his fists ready to hit her. Mum put her hands over her face and screamed.

That was when I attacked him. I couldn't just sit there and watch him beat up my mum. I charged into the man. I was lucky. He hadn't been expecting any trouble from me. I was just a kid. He didn't think I'd be any bother.

I hit him in the side and he lost his balance. His arms wheeled in the air as he fell backwards. His back whammed into the wall outside the flat, and all his breath was knocked out of him.

Before he could do anything else, I slammed the door shut. I turned the key in the lock and slid the bolts across the bottom and top.

The man hammered on the door with his fists. He shouted at us. He told us we'd really done it now, we'd made a big mistake, we shouldn't have made him angry. He was going to get us. He would break the bloody door down if he had to.

After a while, he stopped shouting. He must have known he wasn't going to be able to bust down the door. Also, he was making a lot of noise. Someone in one of the other flats might hear and contact the police.

We heard him say, "OK. Never mind. You're not important. It's Mick we're after. And we'll find him. You mark my words.

Wherever he is, we'll find him. Mr Mullen doesn't let eight grand go that easily."

Then we heard his footsteps going away down the corridor.

As soon as there was no more noise from outside, my mum started to cry.

I went and hugged her.

"Are you all right, Mum?" I asked.

She nodded and blew her nose. "I'm not hurt. But what if he comes back? What then? Oh Jack, I'm so scared! I don't feel safe here any more. I don't know what to do."

It made me angry to see her so upset. I wanted to do something about it. I wished I could somehow go to Tony Mullen and tell him to keep away from us.

But Mullen always had bodyguards around him. They were big muscle-men like the man who'd just left. It wasn't easy to go and visit him. More likely it was *him* who came and visited you.

I knew too that Mullen wouldn't listen to me. A man like him wasn't going to do what a fifteen-year-old kid asked him to.

I didn't sleep well that night. I tossed and turned in bed. I kept trying to think of a way to fix our problems.

In the morning, there was a card on the doormat. It came with the rest of the post – the junk mail and all those bills which my mum couldn't afford to pay.

The card said –

Trouble Fix Ltd

Those were the only words on it. Under them there was a phone number.

Trouble Fix? I thought. *What the hell can that mean?*

I wanted to know more. And I was desperate. Could the card be the answer to my worries?

Mum and I *were* in trouble, after all, and we needed some way to fix it.

I rang the phone number on the card while Mum was in the shower.

A few hours later, I was in an office in a tall building on the west side of town, and I was being handed a gun.

Chapter 4
Fred Herring

The man behind the desk told me his name was Fred Herring.

"That's a joke, right?" I said. "That isn't your real name."

"I'm afraid it is. My parents called me Frederick George Herring."

"But didn't your parents know what a weird name that was? Fred Herring, red herring. Did they know what 'a red herring' is?"

"A 'red herring' means a dead end – a trail that goes nowhere," said Herring. "I think my parents knew what they were doing. But they had a nasty sense of humour."

"You must have had a hard time at school," I said.

"I did," he muttered, a little sadly. "But let's not talk about me." He rapped the top of the desk, which was one of those cheap flat-pack Ikea ones that you put together yourself. Everything in his office looked like that, except the computer, and that looked about a hundred years old. "How can I help you, young man?"

"Well," I said, slowly, "I got your card in the post this morning."

"Ah, so sending out all those cards has worked. It got me a client. That's good," Fred Herring murmured.

"I think there might be something you could do for me," I went on. "I don't know. We've got a bit of a tricky problem, me and my mum."

"Tell me more."

Herring put his fingers together and bent his head to one side. He had neat, curly grey hair and he was wearing a black polo-neck jumper. He looked and sounded a bit like a vicar.

I told him all about Dad and the loan from Tony Mullen, and about the man who'd come to our flat yesterday.

"So it would make your life better if this Mullen person just 'vanished', wouldn't it?" Herring said.

"Eh? You mean 'vanished' as in ...?" I began to say.

"As in killed," Herring put in for me.

I gave an uneasy smile. "Well, yeah, that would work," I said. "But killing him's going a bit too far, don't you think? There must be something else you could do. Something that isn't so ... drastic."

"But you agree, Jack – no Tony Mullen equals no £8,000 debt and no more visits from nasty men with missing teeth."

"Sure. But –"

"Then let's get rid of him."

Herring said this as if getting rid of Mullen was the simplest thing in the world.

"You don't understand," I said. "Mullen's a gangster. He's got all these goons with him all the time. His flat has a million security alarms. You can't just *get rid of* a man like him. It's impossible."

"Nothing's impossible, Jack," said Herring. "if you plan it right, you can do anything. That's what Trouble Fix Ltd is all about.

That's why I set up this company in the first place. So that my clients can do anything. Anything they want."

"Then ... you *can* deal with Tony Mullen? You can find a way of making him vanish?"

"Not me, Jack."

"What? What do you mean? Are you saying *I've* got to make him vanish?" I laughed. What sort of a joker was this?

"No, not that."

Herring sat back in his chair.

"In cases like these," he went on, "the best thing to do is to set up a problem swap. We can *exchange* problems."

I frowned. "I don't understand," I said.

"Let's say I have another client who's in trouble too, much like you are," Herring said. "Let's say it would help that client if the person who's bothering *him* was no longer around. But what can he do? If my client hurts the other person, everyone know's he's done it. It's obvious. The truth will come out. He can't get away with it. The two of them, him and the person who's bothering him, are linked."

"So, like, if I did something to Mullen, everyone would know it was me," I said.

"That's right."

"But Mullen has lots of enemies. I'm sure there are loads of people who wouldn't mind taking a crack at him, if they could."

"I agree. But even with a long list of suspects, the police would find the killer in the end. They'd know it was you."

Herring bent forward.

"But how would they find someone who has *no* links with Mullen?" he said. "They wouldn't suspect someone who's never heard of Tony Mullen before. Someone who's never had any dealings with the man."

I was beginning to see what Herring was getting at. A light was dawning in my head.

An exchange of problems. A problem swap.

"So ..." I said, "this other client goes after Mullen. And I go after the person *he* wants to get rid of."

"Bingo," nodded Herring.

It seemed insane. I could only just believe it. Should I even be listening to Herring? Should I get up and walk out of his office right away? Somehow I couldn't do it. I wanted to stay put and hear some more.

Herring went on. "There's a client we've got at the moment who's a businessman. He's being blackmailed by a banker. The banker knows the businessman has done some very dodgy deals in the last few years – things that the tax men would be very interested to know about. The banker's told my client that he'll go to the police *and* tell the tax men what he knows. That is, unless the businessman comes up with a big sum of money. He's asked for around £100,000, I believe."

"Whoa," I said.

"Whoa indeed. So I've agreed to help him out, and he'll pay me a quarter of that amount. And this is where you come in."

Herring pointed at me, in case I didn't know who he meant.

"And do you know what the beauty of this is, Jack?" he said. "I'm not going to charge you a penny. The businessman is paying me plenty, and I reckon the world will be a better place without the likes of Tony Mullen in it. So, for the good of everyone, you're getting my services for free."

I didn't know what to say. I still couldn't believe what I was hearing.

"Think about it," Herring said. "Think it over for a moment or two."

I thought hard. With Tony Mullen dead, there would be no more debt. My dad would be able to come out of hiding. My mum and I wouldn't have to worry about one of Mullen's gang hurting us.

But murdering someone? Even someone I hadn't met? That was the price I would have to pay to be free of Tony Mullen. It seemed a high price.

But not *that* high.

With Tony Mullen gone, we'd get our lives back.

"I'm going to have to hurry you, Jack," said Herring. "I need an answer quickly. My other client doesn't have much time. He needs to deal with his problem soon if he's to stay out of jail."

I could save my family ... by killing a total stranger. Was it worth it?

"All right," I whispered.

"Sorry, I didn't quite catch that. Say it again."

"All right," I said, more loudly. It sounded as if someone else was saying it, not me.

And that was all it took. That was how I ended up in the bushes, with a gun, waiting for the banker to come home.

Chapter 5

The Shooting

As I got close to him the banker turned. He'd heard the sound of my trainers on the pavement. I was still holding the gun inside my hoodie, hidden.

The banker had his door key in his hand. He was about to put it into the lock.

Seeing a teenage kid coming towards him, he gave me a little smile. I didn't look like I was any problem. Not at first, anyway. Even my hoodie didn't seem to worry him.

But then he must have seen something in my eyes. In the streetlight, I saw his face change. The smile turned into a frown.

But it was too late for him. Far too late.

I lifted the gun. I pointed it at his chest, as Fred Herring had told me to.

"Aim at the biggest bit of the body," Herring had said as he was showing me how to use the gun. He had poked the middle of his own chest. "Here. That way you're less likely to miss. And don't *pull* the trigger, *squeeze* it."

I squeezed the trigger.

Even as I did so, my mind was screaming:

Don't! What are you doing? Are you mad?

But all I could think about was my mum crying, and my dad walking away from our flat forever, and Tony Mullen's man looking at me and going "All right?" in that nasty way before he pushed Mum over onto the floor.

The gunshot was louder than I ever expected. It was like being in the middle of a thunder clap. The gun jumped in my hands. There was a smell like fireworks going off.

The banker grabbed his chest. He let out a weird gasp, as if someone was strangling him. I saw blood.

Then I ran.

I ran as if there was a tidal wave behind me. The wave was chasing me and trying to catch me and crash down on top of me. I ran harder and faster than I ever had before. I ran along street after street, twisting and turning across the city like it was a maze and I was trying to find my way out. I didn't care where I was going. As long as I was going away from the scene of the crime, that was OK with me.

My ears were ringing from the gunshot. My head was spinning. I ran for what felt like an hour. I ran until I couldn't go another step. I ended up in an alleyway in a part of the city I didn't know. I slumped to the ground. My lungs were burning and my legs trembled. The gun was still in my hand.

I sat there for ages, until my heart beat slowed to normal and it didn't hurt to breathe any more.

Suddenly I felt sick. I bent over and threw up.

After a few minutes I tried to get to my feet. It took me two or three goes, but I stood up in the end.

I spotted some wheelie bins nearby. The alleyway was behind a row of shops and fast-food restaurants. I opened the lid of one of the wheelie bins. It was full of empty cartons and rotting food in rubbish bags. I peeled off the parcel tape from the grip of the gun and dropped it in one bin. I dropped the gun in another.

Then I strode out of the alleyway to try and see where I was. I guessed I was about three miles from home. I saw a church steeple and a factory roof a way off. I knew them and I knew where they were. I began to walk.

All the way home I thought, *I have just killed a man, I have just killed a man.* The words rang round and round my head. I had ended the banker's life with a single bullet. I was a killer. A murderer.

I looked into the faces of everyone I walked past. Could they see it in my eyes? Could they tell what I'd just done? Was it obvious? It must be. I felt as if I was carrying a big sign around with me that said THIS BOY JUST SHOT A MAN IN COLD BLOOD.

Then a police car came racing towards me. It had its flashing lights on and the siren was blasting out. I thought it was going to screech to a halt and policemen would jump out and arrest me. I kept close to the wall. I was terrified. My heart was going like a hammer.

But the police car shot past me and carried on along the road till it was out of sight. The policemen inside hadn't even seen me. They were going after someone else. Maybe they were rushing to get to where the banker had died.

It was late when I got home. Mum was fretting. She wanted to know where I had been all evening.

"Do you have any idea what time it is, Jack?" she said. "I've been going out of my mind with worry. I thought something had happened to you. I thought Tony Mullen ..." She didn't finish the sentence. She didn't want to say what she thought Tony Mullen might have done to me.

I pushed past her and went to my room.

I didn't sleep a wink that night. I kept seeing the banker in my head. Again and again I lifted the gun and fired it at him. Again and again he grabbed at his chest and gasped and fell.

I expected that it would be on the TV news the next morning.

"Banker lies shot on his doorstep," the news reader would say.

But there was nothing at all about the shooting on the news. Why? Maybe the police hadn't told the newspapers and TV yet. Maybe they wanted to keep it secret while they looked into the murder.

There was nothing on the news about Tony Mullen being dead, either. *Wasn't that the other part of the deal?* I thought. *When was he going to be shot?*

Perhaps it was only a matter of time.

I tried to act normal. I ate my breakfast, even though I didn't feel like it. I had a shower and got dressed.

The door bell rang, just as I was about to set off for school.

Mum opened the front door.

Two policeman in uniform were standing in the outside.

"Mrs Jennings?" one of them said.

"Yes," said Mum slowly. Her hand flew to her mouth. "Oh God. Is this about Mick? Has something happened to Mick?"

"No, ma'am," said the other policeman. "Is your son Jack home?"

"Yes, he is."

"We'd like to have a word with him, if you don't mind."

Chapter 6
At The Police Station

I was in a small room with two detectives.
One of them was thin and white, with a long
nose and small sharp eyes. He was Detective
Inspector Flanagan. The other was stocky and
black. His face was much kinder and he had
big glasses with thick rims. He was Detective
Sergeant Johnson. A tape recorder was
whirring softly on the table between them
and me. My stomach was one enormous knot
of dread.

"Now come on, Jack," Johnson said. "We have at least three eye-witnesses who saw you running away after the shooting. They saw you had a gun in your hand. Someone else got a clear look at you from out of their front window. They were in a house in the same street as the shooting."

"All of them talked to a police sketch artist about the person they'd seen," said Flanagan. "And the sketch artist drew this."

Flanagan spun a piece of paper towards me across the table. There was a face drawn on it in pencil. It was of a boy wearing a hoodie. He did look a lot like me.

"It didn't take us long to work out who the boy in the sketch was," said Johnson. "One of our officers works on your estate. She took one look at the sketch and said it was you."

"She also said you were a good kid," said Flanagan. "She said your parents fight a lot, but you've always been OK and kept out of trouble. She had no idea how you could have ended up with a gun. Let alone how you could have used it on someone. She told us you just weren't the type. But I suppose she was wrong, eh?"

"Tell us why you did it, Jack," said Johnson. "Come clean. Tell us everything. What have you got against the man you killed? What did he do to you? And where's the gun now?"

"You'll still be going to prison, even if you do confess and tell us everything," said Flanagan.

"Young offender institution, not prison," said Johnson.

"Sorry," Flanagan muttered. "Not prison, young offender institution. As I was saying, if you do confess, your sentence won't be as long. All you have to do is admit you're guilty and tell us your motive – why you shot the man."

"Come on, Jack. Talk to us. What was it? Were you trying to rob him? We know your family has money troubles. Were you going to mug him? Rich bloke. Perhaps he could spare a couple of hundred quid. But then something went wrong. Maybe he struggled when you tried to take his wallet, and so you got scared and shot him. Is that it?"

I wanted to tell them everything. But my tongue was frozen. My mouth wouldn't work. I couldn't move. I knew my life was over. In a single instant, I'd finished everything. I should never have listened to Fred Herring. I should never have taken the gun. Nothing was going to go right for me ever again. And anything I said now would only make matters worse. So I didn't say a word. I couldn't. What good would it do? None.

"Right, then," Flanagan said at last. He slapped the tabletop with both hands. "That's how it's going to be, eh? You're going to keep your mouth shut. Play the hard man. Fine.

Jack Jennings, I am placing you under arrest for the murder of ..."

His voice faded out. I didn't hear him any more. Everything grew distant around me, as if I was leaving my body and floating away. It didn't matter what Flanagan said. Nothing mattered. My life was over.

Someone led me off to a holding cell in the basement of the police station. The cell had bright white tiles on the walls and a bunk bed in one corner. In the other corner was a toilet. It all stank of cleaning chemicals and old, stale coffee.

They left me there for a long time, alone with my thoughts.

Then they told me I had a visitor.

I thought it must be my mum. She'd come to see me at last. I hoped she had a lawyer with her. Maybe, just maybe, a lawyer could get me out of this mess. But I wasn't counting on it.

But it wasn't my mum.

It was the last person I ever expected to see.

It was Fred Herring.

Chapter 7
Fred Herring, Again

Fred Herring sat down next to me on the bunk. The bunk was the only place in the cell where you could sit, apart from the toilet, which didn't even have a seat.

"First things first," Herring said. "I've got to tell you, I'm impressed, Jack. You actually did it. You shot him. Well done!"

"Well done?" I said, with a scowl. "What do you mean, *well done?*"

"You shot a man at point-blank range. That took guts. Most people would have chickened out, but not you."

"But – but you make it sound like what I did was a good thing," I said.

"Wasn't it?" Fred Herring asked. "You were trying to save your dad and protect your mum. I'd say that was good."

"But he's dead!" I blurted out. "The banker's dead and I'm going to prison for it. And after I get out of prison, I'm going to have a criminal record for the rest of my life. No one will ever give me a job or anything. Most of all when they find out what I was in prison for."

Herring looked at me in an odd way. I would have sworn he was smirking.

"Do you want to know what else impressed me?" he said. "You didn't tell the cops about me and Trouble Fix Ltd. You could have pointed the finger at me and given them my name. After all, it was my idea. But you didn't. Why is that?"

"I dunno," I said with a shrug. "It didn't seem like it would make any difference. It wouldn't change anything. Besides, I'm the one who pulled the trigger. It hardly matters who gave me the gun. *I* did the murder."

Again Herring gave me that odd look. There was something he wasn't telling me, something he knew and I didn't.

"Look up there, Jack," he said.

He pointed to a corner of the cell, high up, near the ceiling.

There was a video camera, just out of reach. I had seen it not long after they put me in the cell. It was a tiny thing with a bright red LED light on the front. The lens was like a cold, black eye looking down at me.

"Do you know what that's for?" he asked.

"Um, to keep a watch on me, I suppose," I said. "Make sure I don't hurt myself. And that no one hurts me. The cops have to be very careful these days."

"That's a good idea. But in fact the camera has been filming you since you got put in here."

"Filming?" I said. It was an odd choice of word to use. "Keeping an eye on me," would have made more sense. Or "carrying out surveillance", maybe. But *filming?*

"Yes," said Herring. "It's been filming everything."

"Wait a second," I said. "How come you know I didn't tell the police about you? In fact, how come you're here at all? If I were you, I wouldn't walk into the cell of someone who could say, 'That's the man who gave me the gun.' It would be a crazy thing to do."

I think I was beginning to understand what was going on. Everything was becoming clear, like a blurry photo coming into focus. *The penny was dropping*, as people say.

But I didn't say out loud what I was thinking. I wanted to hear it from Herring. I wanted to hear the truth coming from his lips.

"We've been filming you ever since you walked into my office, Jack," he said, and he nodded. "There were hidden cameras there. We followed you in secret afterwards. We filmed you outside your flat and also in the street when you were about to kill the banker. There was even a camera when you were with Flanagan and Johnson. Remember those thick glasses Johnson had on? They had a little mini digital camera fitted inside them. It's amazing what you can do with technology these days. We live in a James Bond world."

He scratched the back of his head.

"You see, Jack, we're making a Reality TV show," he said. "Perhaps you've worked that out by now. This has all been a set-up. We're putting ordinary people in extraordinary situations and seeing how far we can push them, how far they'll go. And you're our new star, Jack. You're going to be in our very first episode. Everyone is going to know about you. You're going to be famous!"

Chapter 8
Would You?

It went like this.

There had never been any businessman or banker or blackmail. Herring had made everything up.

The guy I'd shot was a movie stuntman. He was skilled at pretending to die and making it look like it was for real.

There hadn't been any bullets in the gun. They were blanks. They made a lot of noise like real bullets, but were harmless.

The stuntman used a packet of fake blood, hidden under his shirt. He popped it when the gun went off. The blood spattered, just as if a bullet had gone into him.

There was no company called Trouble Fix Ltd. It had been set up for the Reality TV show. There had only been one card sent out too. Herring had lied about that as well. It had been posted through just one letterbox in the entire country, the one at our flat.

Flanagan and Johnson *were* proper police detectives. At least they were real. The police force had agreed to take part in the show because they thought it would be useful. The public would see how easy it was for anyone to end up wanting to murder someone. The police thought this might make people stop and think. And if people thought hard, there might be fewer murders.

"You have your dad to blame for this," Herring said to me. "After your mum chucked him out, he saw an advert we put in the papers. The advert said we were looking for people in trouble so that we could make a programme about them. He got in touch with us and told us about him and Tony Mullen. It was perfect. Just what we were looking for."

"My dad," I said. I didn't understand.

"Yes," said Herring. "By the way, your dad's fine. Safe and well. We've put him up in a nice hotel a long way from here. No one knows where he is except me and a few people from the production team. Tony Mullen definitely doesn't know where he is."

"Well, that's great," I said. "Good for him. Lucky Dad." I was being sarcastic.

Herring told me a bit more about the TV show. It was called *Would You?* and the first episode, with me in it, was going to be on TV in a month. The makers of the show were sure it was going to be a massive hit.

Oh, and one more thing. Fred Herring wasn't his real name after all. His real name was Dennis Smith. He was an actor.

Then he offered me a contract. He took it out of the briefcase he had brought with him. The contract was on ten pages of printed paper. I had to sign it or my episode of *Would You?* could not be shown. I had to say I would let the TV network put it on the air.

"This is the crunch," said Smith, the man who I'd thought was Fred Herring. "This is what it all comes down to, Jack. We're offering you £20,000. That's what we'll pay if you let us use you on the show. You're still a kid – a minor, so the money will go to your parents, not you. But just think. With £20,000, your dad can easily pay off his debt to Tony Mullen, and there'll be more than £10,000 left over. Think what your family could do with all that dosh. It's the offer of a lifetime!"

He was right, of course. My family needed the money. We had to have the money.

There was no choice. I read through the contract and signed it.

Then I left the police station and went home. I was boiling with anger and confusion inside.

My mum knew about everything that had happened. Smith had come to talk to her and filmed it all while I was still at the police station. She was excited at the thought of being on TV and at the idea of the money we were going to get. She was really happy I'd signed the contract.

"Now everything's going to be all right," she said. "I've spoken to your dad on the phone. We had a nice chat. He's going to come home soon, and he's promised to stop gambling. I think he means it this time. We can breathe easy, Jack. We can live again. Everything's going to be all right!"

"But is it, Mum?" I said to her. "Is it?"

Chapter 9

Fame

A month later, my life became hell.

The first episode of *Would You?* was shown at 9 o'clock on a Friday night. It was a prime-time slot. It got 12 million viewers.

One moment, I was a nobody. The next moment, half the country had heard of me. I was the kid who had been ready to commit murder so as to save his family. In the programme, they showed me shooting the banker over and over again. They ran the

film footage at least twenty times. Again and
again the cameras showed how I'd "killed"
him – from several different angles, at
ordinary speed and in slow motion.

That whole weekend, the phone never
stopped ringing. Friends and family called up,
and so did a lot of TV people from London.
They wanted me on their shows. I wasn't
interested.

We couldn't go anywhere, my dad, my
mum and me. There was a mob of reporters
outside the flat. They all wanted to talk to
me. We couldn't set foot outdoors without a
hundred camera flashes going off and a
hundred voices shouting out my name. It
sounded like a pack of wolves howling.

By Sunday, most of the reporters had
drifted away. They'd gone to look for some
other news story.

But I got the piss taken out of me at
school on Monday. My friends couldn't

believe what I'd done. They looked at me as if I was someone else. Some of the kids thought I was pretty cool, but a few were shocked and wouldn't go near me. I felt like some kind of freak.

The school bullies wanted some action now. Before, they'd never bothered me. I was a nobody. Now that I was famous, they wanted to beat me up so that they could be famous too.

"Not so tough without a gun in your hand, eh?" one of the bullies said. He tripped me up outside the science block. He kicked me a few times. "Isn't that right, Mister Big Television Star?"

The bully's mate filmed it all on his camera-phone. He sent the videos around to everyone he knew. Suddenly, I was a victim of a "happy slapping", as well as everything else.

Over the next few weeks I couldn't walk down a street without some stranger yelling at me. They said things like, "Hey you! Killer boy! Hope you haven't got your gun on you!" Or, "Run! Take cover! He's going to shoot!" It drove me nuts.

But the worst thing that happened was when I was walking home across the estate one afternoon. This big black 4-by-4 pulled up beside me. I had heard it coming from a long way off. Its engine didn't make any noise but the hip-hop on the stereo was turned up to maximum volume. I heard the *thunka-thud-thud* of the music for a full minute before the car got to me.

The 4-by-4 had bull bars on the front and all of its windows had black tinted glass, so you couldn't see who was inside.

But I knew who was inside the car.

One of the back windows slid down. The music roared out, then got suddenly quiet. The driver had turned the volume down.

A man leaned out from the back seat and peered at me.

"You're Jack Jennings, ain't ya?"

"Yeah."

"Know who I am?"

I had seen him before around the estate. I knew his face only too well. Everyone on the estate did.

"You're Tony Mullen," I said. My mouth had gone dry and my throat hurt.

"I am," said Mullen.

He rested one arm on the sill of the car window. He had a fat gold Rolex watch on his wrist, and the arm was covered with tattoos all the way from the back of his hand to the rolled-up sleeve of his shirt. He looked hard and grim.

"Seen you on the box, Jack," he said. He rubbed a finger back and forth across his nose. "You were class. The way you handled the gun. And the way you never said a word while the cops were talking to you. Very cool. No mistakes there."

"Thanks," I replied. It seemed a stupid thing to say, but I couldn't come up with anything else.

"Yeah," said Mullen. "So, was it me you wanted dead? When you agreed to kill the other geezer, was the other half of the deal that *I* would get whacked?"

"What? Erm, no. Of course not."

"You sure? Because on that show, you and that bloke in the office were talking about someone who your dad owed money to. You used a name a few times, only it got bleeped out every time. Who could that have been, I wonder. Did your dad owe money to someone else?"

"Yeah," I said. I was desperate. I'd have come up with any lie, in order to get away quickly. "That's right. It wasn't you we were talking about. Someone else. Really."

"Really? Interesting. To be honest with you, I don't mind if it *was* me. I've got paid now. I've got my money back off your dad. I don't hold a grudge. I'd just like to know the truth."

"That is the truth," I said.

Mullen looked hard at me for a while. His face was blank. Then he lifted his hand up. His thumb was up and his forefinger out, to make the shape of a gun.

"Bang," he said.

I jumped.

He laughed.

"You're a rubbish liar, Jack, you know that?" he said. "Lucky for you they did bleep out my name. Otherwise that wouldn't have been a finger I was pointing at you just now. It would have been something a whole lot bigger and made of metal. If you get my drift."

I gulped and nodded.

Mullen smiled. "Tell you what, though. Like I said, you handled the shooting well. I've got to give you credit for that. So if you need a job later – you know, when you leave school – you come to me. I'll sort you out. I could do with a bloke like you on my team."

He grinned again. There was a tiny diamond set into one of his front teeth. It winked in the sunlight.

"Think about it," he said, and the window slid upwards. The 4-by-4 purred away. The hip-hop started hammering again.

That was all I could take. That did it. I'd had enough. I had been made to look a fool on television. I had been beaten up at school. At the police station I'd been worried about having a criminal record for the rest of my life. But what had happened was worse, in a way. From now till I died, people would know me as the Reality TV killer. I would never escape that. And men like Tony Mullen would think I was one of them.

My life was changed forever, and someone would have to pay.

Chapter 10
London

I found out the name of the producer of *Would You?* The producer was the man who had come up with the idea for the show in the first place. He was Paul Vernon. He ran a TV production company down in London. Dennis Smith, also known as Fred Herring, was just the front man, just someone doing a job. Paul Vernon was the brains behind it all. He was the one to blame for everything that had happened to me.

I saw Vernon on a chat show one evening. He was talking to Jonathan Ross. He gave a smug laugh about how well *Would You?* was going. He talked about me with a sneer in his voice, like I was some kind of sucker.

"That Jack Jennings," he said. "Who'd have thought he'd actually shoot someone? Amazing!"

I got a train to London. I told Mum and Dad I was going to stay with a friend there for a few days. They didn't ask too many questions. They didn't even ask who the friend was. That was just as well because I'd made him up. In fact, I'd booked a room in a cheap hotel near Notting Hill Gate.

Mum and Dad didn't much care what I got up to any more, because they were too thrilled about their money. They were spending it like there was no tomorrow. Our flat was full of new stuff. There was hardly room to move, what with the widescreen TV and the huge stereo and the boxes of shoes and all the other things they'd splashed out on.

It was as if Mum and Dad had won the lottery or something. I hadn't seen them this happy in ages. I hated them for it. If they carried on spending as madly as this, pretty soon they would run out of money and end up back in debt. That would serve them right, I thought.

I found the offices where Vernon had his production company. For three days in a row I watched him come and go. I worked out his routine. I knew what time he got into work, what time he left.

One evening, I knew I couldn't wait any longer. It was time to act.

I had a gun. I'd got it from Tony Mullen, who else? I'd sold my brand new PlayStation and bought the gun with the money from that. Mullen had looked pleased as he handed the gun to me.

"Good lad," he had said with a wink. Then he gave me some bullets. "These aren't blanks," he said. "These are the proper job. The real deal."

I skulked outside Vernon's office. I hid in the shadow of a doorway on the other side of the road. It was 6 p.m. Mostly Vernon left for home in a taxi at around 6.15 p.m.

The gun was heavy and cold in my hand. This time I wasn't nervous, like I had been outside the banker's house. I felt no fear at all. I only felt sure that this was the right thing to do. Deep down, solid sure.

Tonight I was *really* going to kill someone I had never met.

Barrington Stoke would like to thank all its readers for commenting on the manuscript before publication and in particular:

Lucy Baker

Jake Barnes

Amy Barton

Shanice Bindley

Adam Bowes

David Brett

Mrs Carter-Brown

Daniel Gibson

Craig Gorman

Elliot Halidu

Chrystal Hall

Kelly Hayes

Kirsten Heywood

Shaun Hicks

Alan Huitson

Vivek Jeromias

Kathleen Keogh

Nathan Keys

Dikiran Kular

Bethany Masson

Zak Millard

Tara Peters

Suzanne Prescott

Emma Preston

Ben Pringle

Jakob Ricketts

Brad Sewell

Alex West

Become a Consultant!

Would you like to give us feedback on our titles before they are published? Contact us at the email address below – we'd love to hear from you!

info@barringtonstoke.co.uk
www.barringtonstoke.co.uk